This igloo book belongs to:

....

igloobooks

Published in 2016
by Igloo Books Ltd
Cottage Farm
Sywell
NN6 0BJ
www.igloobooks.com

LEO002 0116
4 6 8 10 9 7 5 3
ISBN 978-1-78343-590-6

Written by Alice King
Illustrated by Lee Holland

Printed and manufactured in China

Just You and Me

Alice King ❄ Lee Holland

igloobooks

Little Bear was bored with his home in the snow.
There was nothing to do and nowhere to go.
Then, one day

"Post!"

cried Seagull, as he delivered a letter.

Little Bear read it and began to feel better.

Big Bear wrote, "I'm coming to stay."

He arrived by boat the very next day.

"Sorry," said Little Bear, "there's nothing to do."

"There is just snow and ice here and me and you."

"There is **always** fun to be had," said Big Bear.

"It's simply a matter of finding out where."

So, the two bears climbed up a slippy snow mound.

At the top, Big Bear looked all around.

Then he counted, "One, two, three."

He smiled and said, "Follow me!"

They tumbled...

...and flipped.

"Whoo-hoo, we're flying!"

giggled Little Bear, until...

They slid onto the **ice** at the bottom of the hill.

"What fun!" cried the bears,
making slippy bear tracks.
Then, all of a sudden, came a very loud...

CRACK!

Big Bear and Little Bear
scrambled for the side.

Their soft paws skidded and
they began to glide.

Round and round they spun and twirled,
like skating snow bears as they whirled.

They landed in a tangle and Big Bear said,

"Let's play some more before it's time for bed."

They dived under the sea...

...and surfed on the waves.

They played hide-and-seek in magical ice caves.

The bears had such fun together
playing in the snow.

Then the sun went down
and the sky began to glow.

"It's magic,"

Said Little Bear, holding Big Bear's paw.

"I've never noticed these wonderful things before."

"It's been so much
fun today," Little Bear said.
"I told you so," said Big Bear,
stroking his head.

The bears curled up in the soft moonlight.
"Thank you, Big Bear," said Little Bear.
"Goodnight."